BATMAN™ BATTLE IN THE BATCAVE

BY DONALD LEMKE
ILLUSTRATED BY ANDIE TONG

Batman created by Bob Kane

HARPER FESTIVAL
An Imprint of HarperCollinsPublishers

THE VILLAINS AND HEROES
IN THIS BOOK!

BANE

Raised inside the walls of a prison, Bane grew into one of Gotham City's strongest and most intelligent criminals. Destroying the Dark Knight is his ultimate goal.

HarperFestival is an imprint of HarperCollins Publishers.

Batman: Battle in the Batcave
Copyright © 2014 DC Comics.
BATMAN and all related characters and elements are trademarks of and © DC Comics.
(s14)
HARP30564

Manufactured in China.
For information address HarperCollins Children's Books, a division of HarperCollins Publishers, 195 Broadway, New York, NY 10007.
www.harpercollinschildrens.com
Library of Congress catalog card number: 2013937488
ISBN 978-0-06-220998-6

14 15 16 17 8 SCP 10 9 8 7 6 5 4 3 2 1
❖
First Edition

BATMAN

Orphaned as a child, young Bruce Wayne trained his body and mind to become Batman, the Dark Knight. He is an expert martial artist, crime fighter, and inventor. Using high-tech gadgets and weapons, Batman fights against the most dangerous criminals in Gotham City.

ROBIN

Robin is Batman's teenage crime-fighting partner. As a child acrobat, this Boy Wonder learned the high-flying skills required to soar alongside the Dark Knight.

COMMISSIONER GORDON

James Gordon is the Gotham City Police Commissioner. He works with Batman to stop crime in the city.

On a cold winter night, an explosion shakes the streets of downtown Gotham City. Within moments, police cars flood the scene with their red-and-blue lights.

Commissioner James Gordon and several other officers quickly exit their vehicles. Near a burning building stands a large, masked figure. "Freeze!" shouts Gordon.

The flames grow brighter, and the man steps closer. "But things are just heating up, Commissioner," the man says.

Suddenly, from high above the city, Batman swoops to the ground on his Batrope. He lands in front of his worst enemy. "Bane," the hero grumbles.

"You remember me, Batman," says the super-villain.
"Unfortunately, you will soon be forgotten."
Bane leaps at the Dark Knight with all his might. The hero
easily dodges the hulking brute using his expert martial arts skills.

Batman snatches a bola from his Utility Belt. He twirls
the weapon above his head and then flings it at Bane.

The rope twists around the villain's ankles, sending him to the ground with
a loud thud. "The bigger they are, the harder they fall," says the hero.

A thick cloud of smoke fills the air. Batman is blinded. When the smoke clears, the cover of an open manhole rests on the street in front of him. Bane is gone!

Days later, Batman sits inside the Batcave. The top secret hideout is hidden deep below Bruce Wayne's mansion. It contains hundreds of gadgets and weapons, as well as Batman's collection of crime-fighting evidence.

The Dark Knight stares at a map on the Batcomputer. "Bane couldn't have gotten far," he says. "The sewer pipes are dead ends, except for the one leading here."

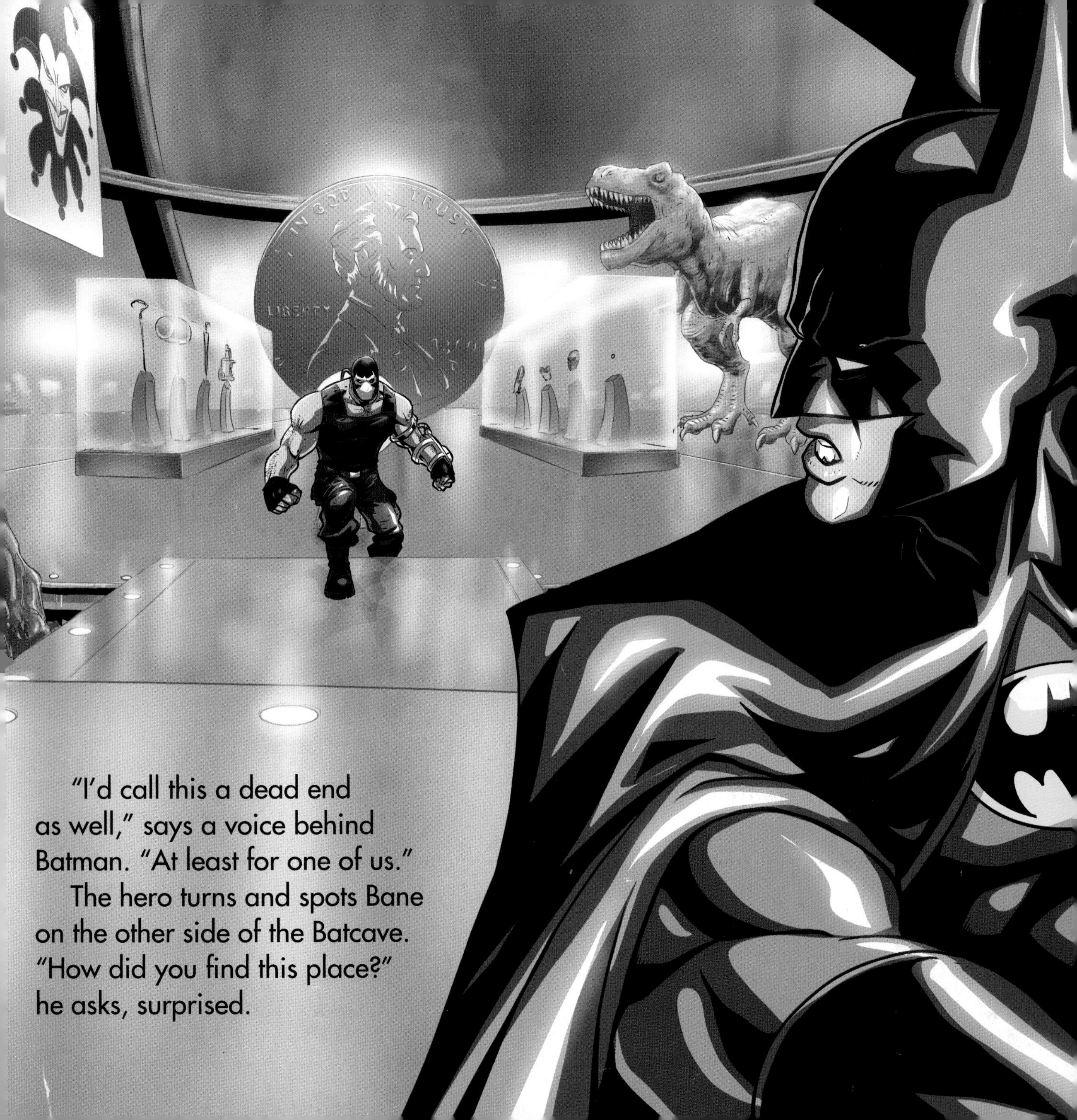
IN GOD WE TRUST

"I'd call this a dead end as well," says a voice behind Batman. "At least for one of us."

The hero turns and spots Bane on the other side of the Batcave. "How did you find this place?" he asks, surprised.

"A few days in the dark and you learn to follow your instincts," Bane replies. "Like a bat, I suppose."
"This cave only has room for one," says Batman.

"How about we flip for it?" suggests the villain. With unmatched strength, Bane lifts Batman's giant penny into the air. He hurls the two-ton coin at the hero.

The Dark Knight avoids the giant penny, and it crashes into a glass display case. The weapons of a dozen criminals spill onto the floor.

Bane grabs the Penguin's umbrella off the ground. He presses a button on the handle, and a fireball explodes from the high-tech weapon.

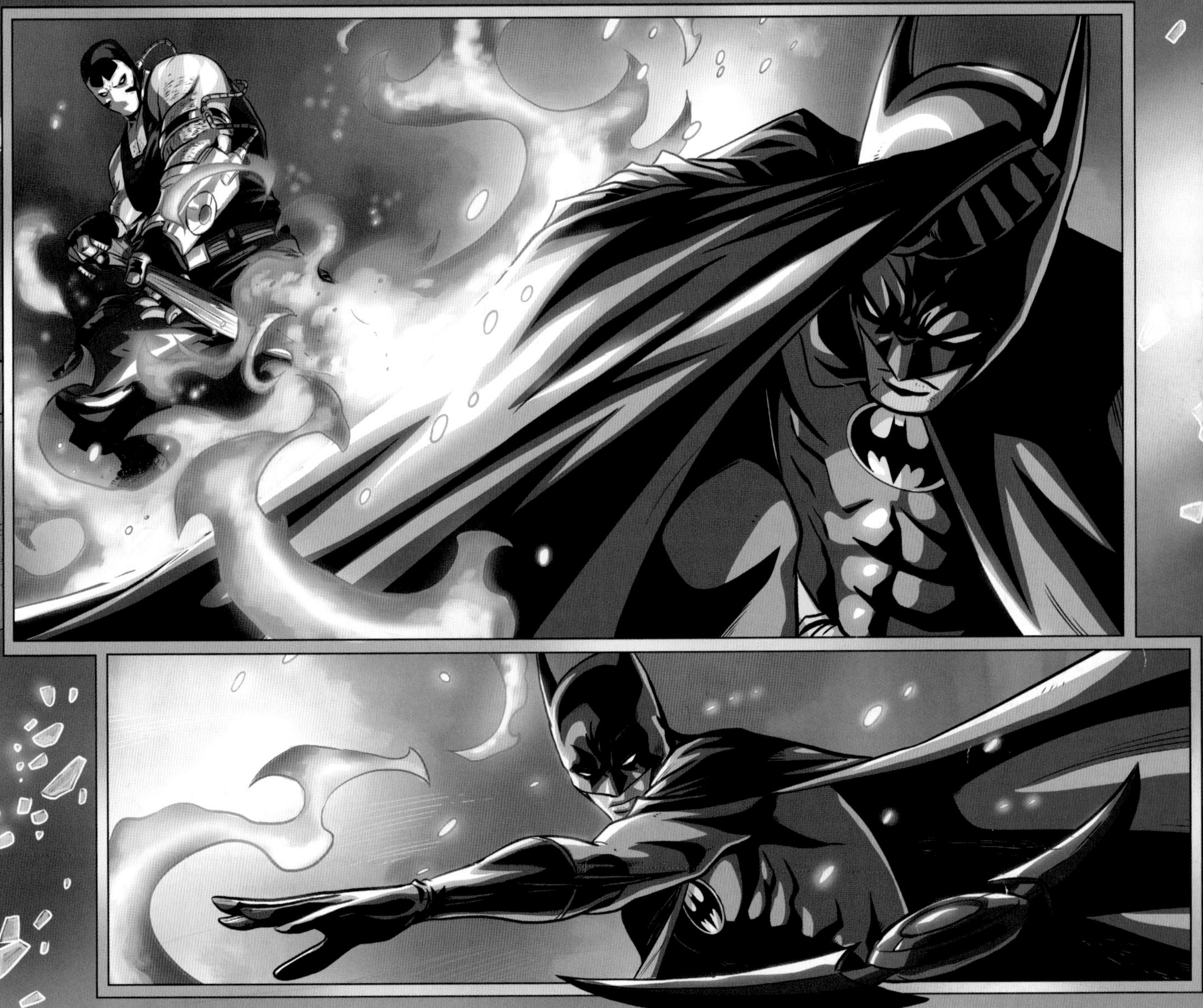

Batman blocks the flame with his fireproof cape. Then he flings a Batarang at the villain, who swats away the metal weapon like a moth.

Bane tosses the umbrella aside and picks up a question-mark cane.
The weapon once belonged to Gotham's cleverest crook, the Riddler.
"Riddle me this," Bane jokes. "How did the bat feel when he lost his cave?"

"Shocked!" Bane quickly answers. He fires an electric bolt at Batman. The bolt strikes the hero! Electricity jolts through his body, stunning him.

Then Bane grabs another weapon from the floor. The Joker's
mallet! "Looks like I'll have the last laugh today," he jokes.
  The villain swings the mallet at Batman. The dazed super hero
dodges the blow. Bane swings and misses, again and again.

"Strike three!" shouts a voice. On the other side of the Batcave stands Robin, Batman's teenage sidekick. He holds Mr. Freeze's ray gun.

Bane lowers the mallet and turns toward Robin. "Where are your manners, Boy Wonder?" he says. "Don't you know better than to interrupt grown-ups?"

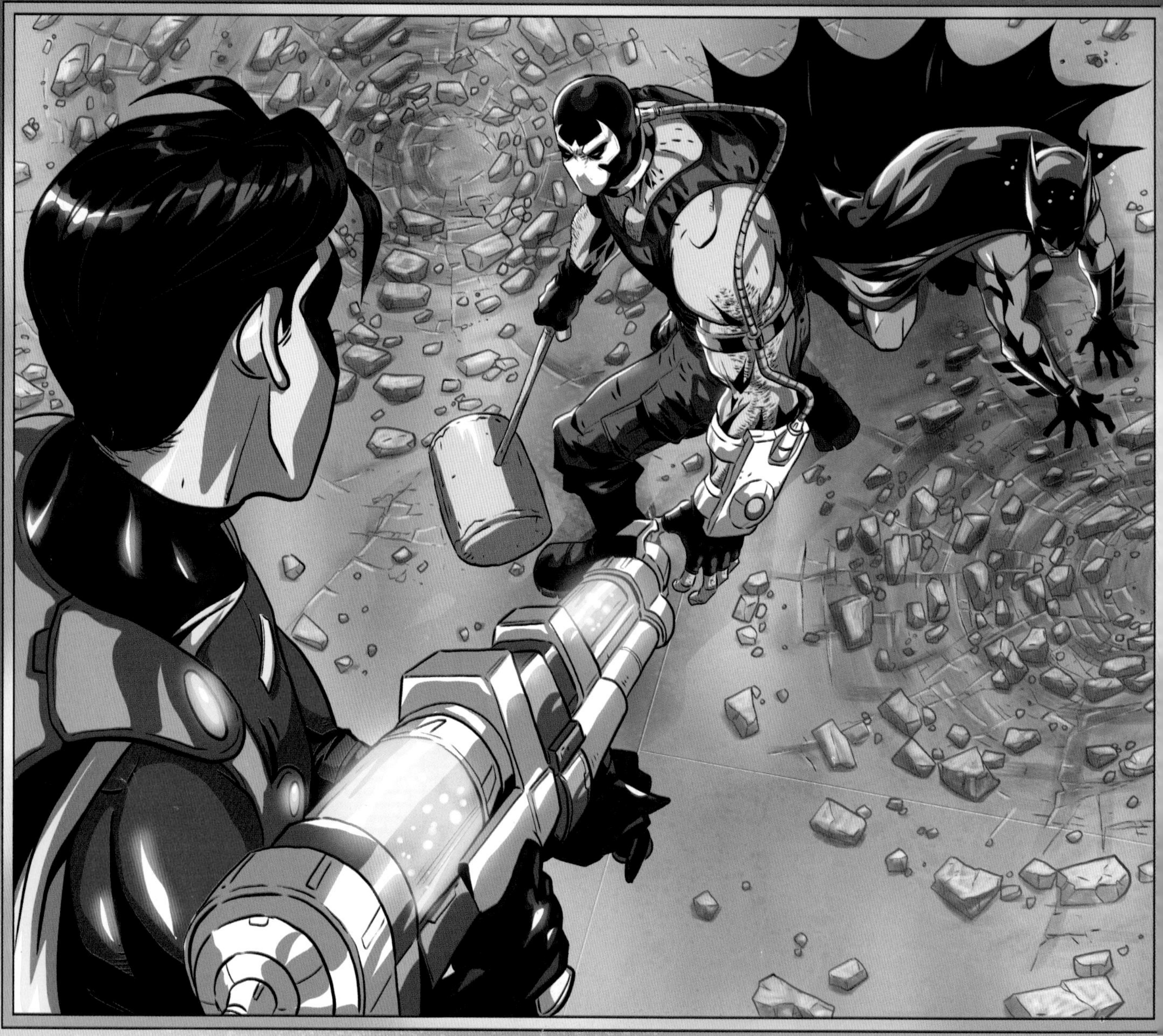

Robin raises the freeze gun. "For a cold-blooded crook, you're a real hothead," says the teenage sidekick. "Time to chill out." The Boy Wonder fires an icy blast at the super-villain.

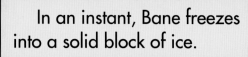

In an instant, Bane freezes into a solid block of ice.

Batman thanks his young partner. "You never were an early bird," the hero jokes. "You're right, Batman," Robin agrees, "but I always catch the crook."

Later at Arkham Asylum, the Dynamic Duo meets with James Gordon. "Great work, you two," says the commissioner. "Bane doesn't remember a thing, but he'll have plenty of time to think in here."

"Sounds like a bad case of brain freeze, if you ask me," Robin says with a smile. The Batcave's location is secret once again.